The Great Gerbil Roundup

The Great Gerbil Roundup

by
Stephen Manes

Illustrated by
John McKinley

Harcourt Brace Jovanovich, Publishers
San Diego   New York   London

Requests for permission to make copies of any part of the work should be mailed to: Permissions, Harcourt Brace Jovanovich, Publishers, Orlando, Florida 32887.

Library of Congress Cataloging-in-Publication Data
Manes, Stephen, 1949-
The great gerbil roundup.
Summary: In an effort to put the town of Gerbil, Pennsylvania on the map, the residents open up The First National Drive-Thru Museum of American Sightseeing and Clean Rest Rooms and stage a gerbil roundup and jubilee.
[1. City and town life—Fiction. 2. Humorous stories] I. Title.
PZ7.M31264Gr 1988   [Fic]   88-2266
ISBN 0-15-232490-9

Designed by Nancy J. Ponichtera
Printed in the United States of America
First Edition
A B C D E

FOR KEVIN, TIRELESS TOURIST

1

WELCOME TO GERBIL
AN OKAY PLACE TO LIVE

Elton Wazoo noticed the sign the day he and his dad moved to town. He quickly learned the sign wasn't kidding. Gerbil, Pennsylvania, was a perfectly ordinary little town.

On Saturdays, people got into their cars and drove thirty-three miles to the shopping mall in Wartchester to buy things they couldn't find downtown. On Sundays, people stayed home and watched TV and found out about all the things they hadn't gotten around to buying yet. The rest of the week, people went to work at the gerbil farm or the roller-skate-wheel factory so they could pay for the things they'd bought.

Gerbil was an absolutely ordinary little community. But things began to change when IN-TERPETCO bought the gerbil farm.

The biggest change was the sign atop the barn. The old sign had said **MCGINNITY'S GERBILS** above a little picture of one of the lovable rodents. The new billboard was thirty feet tall and said **MCGINNITY'S GERBILS, A DIVISION OF INTERPETCO** in big neon letters and **GERBIL CAPITAL OF THE WORLD** in even bigger neon letters. It also had an eighteen-foot-tall picture of something that looked like the host of a TV quiz show but was supposed to be a gerbil in a three-piece suit. INTERPETCO liked to do things in a big way.

It was Elton's dad who came to run the place. Mr. Wazoo had been with INTERPETCO for years. He had managed a canary farm in the Canary Islands, a turtle farm in Turtle Bay, a chameleon farm in Washington, D.C., and an alligator ranch in New York City. He had been everywhere and had seen everything. He liked new challenges. He had big ideas. And he wasn't afraid of sharing them.

"Ladies and gentlemen," he told the Gerbil Town Council one evening, "I have a matter I wish to call to your attention. I believe this town is in trouble."

"I knew it!" cried Mrs. Curdle, the mayor,

throwing up her hands. "I knew this would happen when your company bought out Old Man McGinnity."

"Hear, hear," cackled Old Man McGinnity. He stroked Lonesome Lucy, the gerbil he always carried around on his shoulder. He stared at Mr. Wazoo.

Mr. Wazoo continued bravely. "The trouble with this town is that it's so ordinary no one's ever heard of it. We need something that will put us on the map."

One of the councilpersons sprang from his seat. "Why, I've been saying that for years! And I have the perfect solution! A donut museum! Picture it! The history of donuts! The science of donuts! Donuts through the ages! Donuts: Man's Gift to Mankind, or Mankind's Gift to Man? The Hall of Famous Donuts. How Donuts Are Made. Donuts in Art, Music, and Literature. Donuts: The Hole Story. People would flock from miles around to see it. If you're proposing a donut museum, you've got my vote, that's for sure," said Councilman Donati.

Mr. Wazoo nodded politely. "I was thinking of something even more spectacular."

"We could even have a merry-go-round in the shape of a donut," said Mr. Donati. "What could be more spectacular than that?"

"That is exactly what I would like to find out," Mr. Wazoo replied. "I'd like to hold a contest to find the very best idea for a tourist attraction for Gerbil. All our schoolchildren can enter. INTERPETCO will award the winner the pet of his or her choice, and we'll make every effort to make the winning idea a reality. INTER-PETCO wishes to be a valuable member of the community."

"Well, I can tell you what my kids are going to suggest, all right," muttered Mr. Donati.

"I'm sure you can," snorted Mayor Curdle. Then she moved that the council give Mr. Wazoo permission to hold his contest, along with three hearty cheers and the key to the city. The motion passed unanimously.

Mr. Wazoo soon discovered that the key only opened the rest rooms at the mayor's gas station. It was the thought that counted.

2

At first the contest was closed to anyone related to an employee of McGinnity's Gerbils or any other division of INTERPETCO, but that disqualified almost all the kids in town. The rules were changed so that every student in the Gerbil School District could enter—except those who happened to be related to the chief executive of McGinnity's Gerbils, Mr. Dagbert Wazoo. This meant Elton was the only kid in town who couldn't enter the contest. He was made one of the judges, along with Mayor Curdle and Old Man McGinnity.

Elton Wazoo hadn't been terribly popular since he'd moved to Gerbil. It wasn't that the local kids were unfriendly to strangers—just that they'd never met anyone who'd been all over the world before. Most of them thought Elton was showing off when he told them about his adventures in Borneo and Togo and Macao and New Jersey. They got very tired of hearing about what a wonderful animal trainer Elton's mom was. And they especially hated it when Elton would frown about something and proclaim, "They do this a lot better in Zamboanga." But he couldn't help it. They really did do some things a lot better in Zamboanga.

However, as a judge for the great tourist-attraction contest, Elton became one of the most important people in town. Kids suddenly stopped calling him "Zamboanga Wazoo." Some asked him for advice about how to win. Others tried to bribe him. One or two threatened to beat him up if they didn't get the prize.

Elton patiently explained to one and all that every entry would come to him without names, that he would vote for the best one no matter what, and that his vote was only one out of three anyhow. So anybody who planned to beat him up had better plan to beat up Old Man McGinnity and Mayor Curdle, too. Since Old Man McGinnity was the town's champion arm-wrestler and Mayor Curdle weighed two hundred eighty-six pounds in her gas-station uniform, that put an end to that.

On the day of the judging, Elton was locked in the council chamber with Mayor Curdle, Old Man McGinnity, Lonesome Lucy, and all the contest entries. Each judge took a stack of entries and separated it into two piles: good ideas on the right, bad ones on the left. Into Elton's left-hand pile went five suggestions for a drive-in Gerbilburger restaurant, four for a shopping mall in the shape of a gerbil, three for a Roller-Skating Hall of Fame, two for a giant statue of a gerbil, one for a bike rack in the city park, and six for a Museum of the Donut—not to mention the ideas of the very littlest kids, such as "a big tree," "a huge fig newton," and "a special magnet that attracts tourists." Elton began to wonder if he would ever be able to start a right-hand pile.

The other two judges were having the same problem. Neither one had a single entry in the good-idea pile. Then Lonesome Lucy suddenly sailed through the air as Old Man McGinnity jumped up, waved a sheet of paper, and cackled, "Here's our winner!"

He handed the entry to Mayor Curdle. She

read it, smiled, nodded, and passed it on to Elton.

Elton read it and whistled softly. It was a brilliant idea. It was definitely the best idea so far. There was just one problem: It was totally impossible.

"Unanimous?" asked Mayor Curdle. "Do we all agree?"

"Nope," Elton replied. "It won't work."

"Will too!" snorted Old Man McGinnity. "You're outvoted, two to one, fair and square!" Lonesome Lucy chittered her vote, too, even though it didn't count.

Mrs. Curdle unlocked the door and left the room. She matched the number at the top of the winning entry with the number on a list of contestants' names. Then she led Elton and Old Man McGinnity to the Town Hall steps. There was a fine tang of gerbil in the air as Mr. Wazoo took the winner's name from Mrs. Curdle and stepped to the microphone.

The crowd hushed. "We have our winner!" Mr. Wazoo declared. "The name is . . . McBeth McBeth!"

"I knew it!" shrieked a girl in the crowd, shoving people aside as she rushed toward the steps. "I knew I'd win!"

Elton was not the least bit surprised that McBeth was the winner. She was in his class at school, and she was considered rather weird— partly because she kept her glasses on with a plaid elastic glasses-holder and never wore socks that matched, and partly because she was interested in unusual things like architecture and telegraphy and cheese-and-chocolate sandwiches. If there was one thing McBeth had, it was imagination.

Mr. Wazoo congratulated her. "Thank-you," said McBeth McBeth. "For my prize, I would like a rhinoceros."

Elton watched his father turn pale. "We'll discuss those arrangements later," Mr. Wazoo assured her. "Why don't you tell everyone about your prizewinning idea?"

"My prizewinning idea is going to make this town famous!" McBeth beamed. "My prizewinning idea—I just knew I'd win!—is to move Niagara Falls right here to Gerbil!"

3

When he'd recovered from his fainting spell, Mr. Wazoo led Elton and McBeth into the council chambers. "Well," he said, taking a deep breath, "this is quite a tall order."

"Tall order, my elbow," sniffed McBeth McBeth. "Your company can get as many rhinoceroses as it needs."

"I wasn't talking about the rhinoceros. I was talking about your idea of moving Niagara Falls. Elton, sometimes you do get me into the most embarrassing situations."

"This can't be as embarrassing as the time that cheetah ate your pants," Elton said. "Besides, I didn't even vote for it. It was two to one, fair and square. You'll just have to make the best of it."

"Right," McBeth agreed. "Now, what about my rhinoceros?"

"The real question," said Mr. Wazoo, "is how we go about moving Niagara Falls here. It's impossible."

"That's what I thought at first, Dad," Elton said. "But remember that motto above your desk: 'At INTERPETCO, nothing's impossible.' If the country can put a man on the moon, and INTERPETCO scientists can invent a crunchless, dry cat food, maybe you can figure out a way to move Niagara Falls to Gerbil."

"Right," McBeth repeated. "Now, my rhinoceros, please?"

"The prize was a choice of *pet* from INTERPETCO," Mr. Wazoo informed her. "Rhinoceroses are not pets."

"They are to me. And I know for a fact that INTERPETCO has a rhinoceros department: Rory Rallickson's Rhinoceros Ranch, a division of INTERPETCO."

"Strictly speaking," replied Mr. Wazoo, "that is not an INTERPETCO company. It's a division of WILDBEASTIECO."

"Which is a division of INTERPETCO,"

McBeth pointed out. "Same difference. Are you going to give me my rhinoceros or not?"

"I'll need a note from your parents," said Mr. Wazoo.

McBeth reached into her pocket and handed him a piece of paper. It read:

To whom it may concern:
We have no objection whatsoever if our daughter owns a rhinoceros.

Sincerely yours,
Joe and Lady Bird McBeth

Mr. Wazoo's brow became somewhat moist. "You know, a rhinoceros really wasn't intended as a prize. How about a beautiful platypus instead?"

"It's a rhinoceros, or I sue," said McBeth. "And I probably don't have to remind you that the town judge is my Uncle Duncan."

Mr. Wazoo leaned back in his chair and thought for a long while. "I'm sure you know there's a law against keeping rhinoceroses within the Gerbil town limits."

McBeth had forgotten. *Uh-oh*, she said to herself.

"Certainly there must be something you want more than a rhinoceros," said Mr. Wazoo.

"Well, there is one thing," McBeth said suspiciously. "But it isn't a pet."

"Maybe we can make a trade," said Mr. Wazoo. "What is it?"

"A trip to Niagara Falls," said McBeth.

"It's a deal," replied Mr. Wazoo.

4

McBeth McBeth had two great ambitions: She wanted to become a rhinoceros trainer, and she wanted to see Niagara Falls. She'd been in love with the place ever since the mailman had mistakenly brought her a fold-out postcard with twenty-two full-color views of it. McBeth was sure Niagara Falls had to be the most beautiful natural wonder in America and maybe even the world. She couldn't wait to see if everything looked exactly the way she imagined it.

So when Mr. Wazoo parked the car and McBeth spotted the sign that said **TO THE FALLS,** she ran all the way. She had read every book in the library about the falls. She had seen

hundreds of pictures. But when she reached the brink, she couldn't believe her eyes. Or her ears. More water hurtled over in one second than McBeth had seen in her entire life, and none of the pictures had prepared her for the way it all glittered and roared. Off in the distance, she could see an even bigger waterfall, a huge curved one, and just across the river was Canada. McBeth wanted to take it all home with her.

"My idea was even better than I imagined!" she shouted over the roar when the Wazoos caught up with her. "Won't this look incredible in Gerbil?"

Elton had to agree. He'd seen waterfalls all over the world, but none to top this one. He and McBeth pointed and gawked and marveled at the falls. Mr. Wazoo pulled out his pocket calculator and made a rough estimate of what it would cost to move them.

The mayor of Niagara Falls, New York, had an American eagle above his door, an American flag beside his desk, and an American League baseball schedule on his wall. He was eating an American cheese sandwich when his visitors from Gerbil came through the door.

"We want to buy the falls, and money is no object," Mr. Wazoo declared. "INTERPETCO is one of the seventeen largest companies in Pennsylvania. We offer the nation's most complete selection of pets, and we're a major producer of dog biscuits, cat scratching posts, birdseed, fish food, lunch meats, and frozen ravioli. We have millions of dollars at our disposal."

The mayor looked thoughtful. "The falls have been here a long time. They'll be here for a long time to come."

"False," said McBeth. "The falls are eroding. Falling apart. Heading for Buffalo. Why, the little book I bought in the souvenir stand this morning says that in just a few hundred thousand years, they'll be gone. And Mother Nature won't give you a dime for them. But Mr. Wazoo is prepared to pay you handsomely to take them off your hands."

The mayor put down his sandwich. "Your proposal is not without interest," he said with his mouth full. "I suggest you speak with the mayor of our sister city across the river. Let me know what he thinks of the idea."

Across the river, in Niagara Falls, Ontario, the group from Gerbil rode the *Maid of the Mist*, a little boat that took them right to the very bottom of the Horseshoe Falls. It was thrilling. Rainbows hovered in the mist overhead, and everyone would've been soaked to the skin if the boat company hadn't provided heavy, yellow slickers.

"This will put Gerbil on the map for sure!" McBeth shouted over the water's roar. "You think we'll have to change the name of our town?"

"Maybe!" Elton shouted back. "It certainly wouldn't make sense to call this Gerbil Falls!"

The mayor of Niagara Falls, Ontario, was even friendlier than his counterpart across the river. Beneath the Canadian flag, he munched on a Canadian bacon sandwich and sipped Canada Dry ginger ale while he listened to Mr. Wazoo's offer. Then he leaned across the desk. "I'm highly flattered, but I'm afraid it's out of the question. Do you see this stack of letters?"

He pointed to a pile under a Canada goose paperweight. Mr. Wazoo, Elton, and McBeth nodded.

"These," the mayor went on, "are requests from ordinary Canadian towns asking if we'd mind lending them the falls for a few years. If we lent the falls to one of them, we'd have to lend the falls to all of them, and it's not as if there are enough falls to go around. Now imagine the outcry if we were to sell the falls to an ordinary town in another country. We'd never hear the end of it. Besides, what would we call ourselves if we sold the falls? Nowhereville? Dry Gulch? I'm sorry, but it can't be done."

Mr. Wazoo looked sad. Elton threw up his hands and sighed. McBeth irritably snapped the elastic on her glasses.

"Don't feel too glum about it," said the mayor. "I certainly won't let you go home empty-handed. As a token of international friendship, I would like you to take this home with you." He handed Mr. Wazoo a little bottle filled with a clear fluid.

"Thank you," said Mr. Wazoo. "What is it?"

"A little bit of the falls," said the mayor. "We can't sell you the whole thing, but we're delighted to give you a small part."

"We're very grateful," said Mr. Wazoo.

5

Back home, Mr. Wazoo presented the bottle of Niagara Falls to Mayor Curdle, who was sorely tempted to ask for her rest-room key back. Then INTERPETCO's vice president and general manager in charge of gerbils hid himself in his office and ordered his secretary to tell callers he was on safari in North Dakota. Mr. Wazoo felt he had failed, and he was not used to failure.

In school, a lot of kids snickered at Elton and called him names like "Niagara Wazoo" and "Wazoo Falls"—and worse. But after a while, he began to get used to it. The one person who never said an unkind word to him was McBeth McBeth. She wore a necklace with a little charm of Niagara Falls, carried a notebook that said "I saw Niagara Falls," wore a red sock that said "Niagara" and a green one that said "Falls," blew her nose in a handkerchief with a picture of you-know-what, and punched anybody who even considered sending a snicker her way. Naturally, she and Elton got to be friends.

"My dad's taking this pretty hard," Elton told her. "He really wants to do something for the town. He thinks Gerbil's an okay little place, but he says there's always room for improvement."

"He could build a donut museum," McBeth suggested. "Mr. Donati would give him a lot of help."

"Dad's never been a big fan of donuts," said Elton. "He prefers frozen ravioli."

"Well, nobody's interested in a ravioli museum. Don't you have any other ideas?"

"Not a one."

"Maybe you could open the gerbil farm to tourists."

Elton shook his head. "No chance. INTER-PETCO has an ironclad rule about visitors. The company got kind of upset one time when somebody accidentally left the door to the cheetah farm open. For all we know, there may still be stray cheetahs running loose in Idaho. We never did catch them all."

"Come to think of it, it probably wouldn't work anyhow," said McBeth. "Old Man McGinnity let visitors tour the farm for a while, but people weren't all that interested in seeing more than one or two gerbils at a time. Or smelling them."

"At least we've got part of Niagara Falls," said Elton. "That's something, anyhow. You can go down to Town Hall and see it in the display case for free any time you want to."

"Yeah," said McBeth. "Everybody in town's seen it five or six times already."

"Maybe they'll start charging admission," Elton joked.

McBeth suddenly got an inspired look on her face. "That's it!" she cried. "I've got it! The perfect thing to put this town on the map!"

"I hope it works out better than Niagara Falls," said Elton.

"It can't fail!" cried McBeth.

6

One week later, McBeth invited Elton to come over after school to test her plan on him.

"You are the very first person in the entire world to learn about the tourist attraction that will make Gerbil, Pennsylvania, famous throughout the world. Ta-da!"

And with that fanfare, she flipped back the covering from a gigantic poster. It read:

SEE   **NIAGARA FALLS!**
SEE   **THE GRAND CANYON!**
SEE   **THE STATUE OF LIBERTY!**
SEE   **THE ALAMO!**
SEE   **DISNEYLAND!**

SEE   THE GREAT METEOR CRATER!
SEE   MILWAUKEE!

AND MUCH, MUCH MORE!

SAVE TIME! SAVE MONEY! SAVE GAS!
VISIT THE FIRST NATIONAL
DRIVE-THRU MUSEUM
OF AMERICAN SIGHTSEEING
AND CLEAN REST ROOMS.
ROUTE 272, IN GORGEOUS,
GLORIOUS GERBIL.
PATRIOTIC! CULTURAL! EXCITING!

IF YOU MISS IT, TOO BAD FOR YOU!

"Well, what do you think?" McBeth asked.
Elton shook his head. "I don't know. There sure are a lot of exclamation points. And how do you plan to get all this stuff?"
"All what stuff?"
"All the stuff for the museum. You know we can't get Niagara Falls. And if I remember my geography right, the Grand Canyon won't even fit in Gerbil."
"Aha! Fooled you!"
"What?"

"Come closer."

Elton did.

"Now, look again."

Elton bent over. When his nose was almost touching the poster, he saw what McBeth was talking about. Right between the enormous **SEE** and the enormous **NIAGARA FALLS** were the words "some of" in letters so tiny a flea might have had trouble deciphering them. Indeed, an educated flea would have read a sign very different from the one Elton had seen at first:

SEE some of **NIAGARA FALLS!**

SEE a rock from **THE GRAND CANYON!**

SEE a souvenir replica of **THE STATUE OF LIBERTY!**

SEE an ashtray shaped like **THE ALAMO!**

SEE a Donald Duck T-shirt direct from **DISNEYLAND!**

SEE a hole that resembles **THE GREAT METEOR CRATER!**

SEE a giant beer can from **MILWAUKEE!**

"Well, what do you think?" McBeth demanded.

"It seems a little dishonest," Elton pointed out. "Besides, do you really think people are going to pay to see that stuff?"

"Pay? Who said anything about paying? You don't have to pay to see Niagara Falls, do you?"

"No, but . . . "

"Here's the way I figure it. People do most of their traveling in summer, right? Okay. Usually it gets so hot in the summertime that they'd really rather spend their vacations at home in their backyards sipping a nice cool lemonade or a Dr. Pepper or one of those awful whiskey drinks grown-ups like so much. But everybody else in the neighborhood is taking a trip, so these people figure they have to, too, just to keep up. They drive hundreds of miles in the heat and humidity and traffic and spend a fortune on gas and hotels and lousy hamburgers. And they're miserable.

"But if they come to the First National Drive-Thru Museum of American Sightseeing and Clean Rest Rooms, they can see the U.S.A. without running all over the place. They can drive through and look at all the exhibits in the privacy of their own cars, they can freshen up in the clean rest rooms, and then they can go home and spend the rest of their vacations lying around in the backyard guzzling iced tea while they tell their neighbors how beautiful Niagara Falls was—what they saw of it."

Elton scratched his chin. "Doesn't sound too bad. What about people without cars?"

"We can build a special lane for them. But they have to come in on skateboards or bikes or wagons or wheelchairs or something. No wheels, they're out of luck. Who ever heard of sightseeing on foot?"

"You really have thought this out," Elton said. "Can the museum support itself?"

"We won't charge admission to the exhibits," McBeth explained. "However, there will be a small fee for use of the clean rest rooms."

Elton laughed so hard he nearly fell off his chair. "Brilliant! Magnificent!"

"Glad you think so," McBeth said proudly.

"One more question," said Elton. "Where are you going to get the money to build this thing?"

"That's where I thought you and your dad might come in," said McBeth McBeth.

7

Mr. Wazoo's secretary told everyone her boss was visiting a prairie dog town in Floydada, Texas, but Elton knew better and barged into the office with McBeth. Still feeling terrible over his failure with Niagara Falls, Mr. Wazoo was talking into a microphone, dictating a letter to the president of INTERPETCO. He begged to be transferred to another division— the Guppy Pond, the Kangaroo Korral; he wasn't particular—to spare him the embarrassment of having to face the citizens of Gerbil again.

"I think you're making a bad mistake," Elton told him. "What happened to your Big Ideas?"

Mr. Wazoo looked like a lost puppy. "Vanished," he said forlornly.

"What would Mom think?" Elton asked. Elton's mom wasn't afraid of anything. She worked for INTERPETCO as an animal trainer. At that very moment, she was ten thousand miles away, calming an angry Komodo dragon with carefully chosen words of encouragement.

The company always seemed to assign her to jobs on the other side of the globe, and many people thought it a strange way to run a marriage. To Elton, it was absolutely normal. He spent half his time with his mom, and half his time with his dad, and on the rare occasions both his parents were around, he felt almost smothered with affection.

"Mom would say you're being childish," Elton told his father. "Especially if she saw this great new plan McBeth's worked out."

"No more plans!" cried Mr. Wazoo. "My only plan is to move someplace where they've never heard of Niagara Falls."

"No need," said McBeth. "Ta-da!" She unveiled her poster and explained her proposal before Mr. Wazoo had a chance to object.

Fifteen minutes later, he was convinced. He suggested a few additions and changes, gave McBeth money for more posterboard and markers, and took her proposal to the Town Council the very next night.

"Sure hope this works better than your last plan, Wazoo," said Councilman Donati. "My kids made six excellent suggestions in that idiot contest of yours, and they didn't win a thing."

Mr. Wazoo thanked him politely and began his presentation. First he held up McBeth's sign. Then he unveiled her pictures and diagrams of the museum-to-be. Long lines of cars waited patiently to get in. A family in a station wagon stared goggle-eyed at a kitchen chair almost exactly like the one George Washington had sat on at Valley Forge. Three clean-cut roller skaters marveled at a chocolate angel-food cake in the shape of the Liberty Bell.

But the picture everyone liked best was the one that showed the most brilliant part of McBeth's idea: desperate-looking people handing over fifty cents each to use the rest rooms. The masterstroke was the fine print on the sign beside the door: **TOILET PAPER 25 CENTS EXTRA.**

Most of the councilpersons liked the plan a lot, but there was one who did not. "If you ask me, I don't see how this is anywhere near as interesting as a Museum of the Donut. How can a little bottle of water be more interesting than the history of the donut? How can an old ashtray beat the science of the donut? Who would rather see a dumb old rock than the Hall of Famous Donuts? Who could possibly prefer a hole from a meteor crater—?"

Mr. Wazoo came prepared to deal with this issue. "May I interrupt?" he asked politely.

" — to a hole from a donut? Oh, go ahead, Wazoo."

Mr. Wazoo thanked him. "There is much wisdom in what you say, Honorable Councilman Donati."

Mr. Donati folded his arms and looked at his fellow councilpersons as if to say he'd told them so.

Mr. Wazoo continued. "Donuts have always been an important part of American sightseeing. Why, without the donut, travelers' stomachs might go empty for hours at a time, causing indigestion and accidents. The ad hoc committee for the First National Drive-Thru Museum of American Sightseeing and Clean Rest Rooms has therefore proposed that not only the hole from a typical American donut be enshrined in the museum's permanent collection, but also a donut itself. And, by unanimous agreement, we have selected Donati's Donut Den as our supplier. Will you accept this honor?"

Mr. Donati looked proud but slightly suspicious. "What does this 'ad hoc' mean?"

Mr. Wazoo scratched his head. "Beats me."

Mr. Donati relaxed a little. "What kind of donut do you want? Plain, sugar, chocolate, or jelly?"

"Whichever you feel is most important."

"This is quite an assignment. I'll have to do a lot of research."

"Then you accept?"

"With pleasure. It's not often you meet someone who understands the importance of donuts."

The council briefly debated Mr. Wazoo's proposal. A few of the members wondered whether all the visitors might turn out to be a bad influence on the town, but the other members pointed out that all those visitors would have to eat somewhere, and they'd probably need toothbrushes and dental floss and hair spray and swim fins. So they'd probably spend a lot of money in downtown Gerbil and bring the town a new era of prosperity.

The only other question was whether the museum's toilet facilities might put a strain on the town's sewer system, but Mr. Wazoo guaranteed that his company would take care of any problems that might arise. INTERPETCO would build the museum and use the money from the clean rest rooms to run it. Any leftover profits would be donated to the Gerbil Soothing Music and Cultural Affairs Committee.

The council approved the proposal unanimously and presented Mr. Wazoo with another key to the city. To celebrate, Mr. Donati generously offered everyone present a jelly donut at ten percent off the usual low price.

8

The First National Drive-Thru Museum Et Cetera (as people began to call it) was starting to take shape. INTERPETCO's real estate division bought the ugly old vacant lot at the east end of McGinnity Street and brought in bulldozers to level it off. McBeth drew up the blueprints for the building herself. An architect from INTERPETCO helped fill in the walls, ceilings, and floors of her plans with diagrams of electrical wires, air-conditioning ducts, and plumbing.

Then, to everyone's amazement, Mr. Wazoo appointed Elton and McBeth as chief curators of the museum. They would run the place.

To them, it was a terrific idea, since they'd get to miss a lot of school and earn money to boot. But some townspeople thought it was ridiculous to put two kids in charge of such an important project. Mr. Wazoo calmly stated that he had total confidence in the curators' abilities, and all anyone else could do was grumble.

Joe and Lady Bird McBeth were given time off from their jobs at the gerbil farm and appointed assistant curators. Their job was to drive their young bosses across the country in a special motor home and exhibit collector that the wizards of INTERPETCO's transport division had created from an old elephant van. The Museum-mobile had a rather strong odor at first, but little by little it wore off.

For McBeth, who'd never been anywhere outside Gerbil except for the shopping mall, Knoodler's Grove Amusement Park, and Niagara Falls, the trip was an absolute miracle. She sat glued to the windows for hours, watching scenery and billboards and enormous trucks whiz by, long after Elton got bored and decided to take a snooze or read a book or watch educational TV in the back.

But even Elton, who'd been everywhere, had to admit the trip was one of his best ever. Touring with your parents was one thing, but traveling as the co-curator of an up-and-coming museum was an entirely different experience.

As curators, Elton and McBeth had to keep a constant lookout for interesting and educational exhibits, and there was no telling where they might turn up. On a back road in Wapakawompa, Ohio, McBeth and Elton discovered a six-foot-tall sign in the shape of a perfect ear of corn, and they had to dicker all afternoon before the farmer who owned it would agree to pick it for them. Just off the superhighway near Skaggins, Kentucky, they bought the most perfect diner menu they had ever seen, complete with a roast-beef gravy spot. In Bert, Utah, they found a salt shaker whose contents were guaranteed to have come from the Great Salt Lake.

Outside Cornfed, Kansas, they bagged their first waffle—a round one with star-shaped holes. In Straggler, Wyoming, they found hamburgers so tough the local cowboys used them as soles for their boots. In Terre Haute, Indiana, which means "High Ground, Indiana" in French, they purchased a direct descendant of the world's first French fry. To keep such perishable objects in their original state, they sprayed them with

Eternallife Preservative, a special formula sold only to museums and morticians. It's guaranteed to work in perpetuity or forever, whichever comes first.

McBeth and Elton roamed the countryside and handed out their handsomely engraved business cards, which identified them not as plain old kids but official museum curators with official United States money to spend. Soon their odd-looking and odder-smelling Museummobile grew famous.

People everywhere insisted that Elton and McBeth take something from their town to exhibit. In Mugwump, Minnesota, they were given a spark plug from the first automobile ever to travel from Mugwump to Minneapolis at night. In Hogboro, Missouri, they received a warm welcome and a splintery replica of the nightstick of Police Officer William Organization, inventor of the billy club. In City of Industry, California, they were given a jar of the town's most famous product, but on their way to the next town the lid came loose, and all the smog leaked out.

In Idaho, they bought a potato with eyes that glowed in the dark. They got a cream pie in Boston, cream cheese in Philadelphia, and cheesecake ice cream in Sundae, Wisconsin.

And almost everywhere they went, they received the key to the city. Most of the keys opened nothing more than the restrooms in the mayors' gas stations, but McBeth McBeth kept them in alphabetical order on a huge key ring, and a few times they really came in handy.

At last the Museummobile was so full it wouldn't hold so much as another Silver Dollar Pancake, and the McBeths and Elton headed for home. At the town limits, the sign now read:

WELCOME TO GERBIL
GREAT
AN OKAY PLACE TO LIVE

McBeth kept craning her neck and leaning over, trying to catch a glimpse of the museum. Suddenly it loomed ahead, the building she'd dreamed up, exactly the way she'd imagined it and put it down on paper—only bigger.

McBeth grinned proudly and waved to some workers who were polishing the bricks and painting the trim. Everything seemed perfect until Mrs. McBeth pointed to the roof. Workers there were putting the finishing touches on an enormous sign that shouted **HERE IT IS! MUSEUM! TOILETS!** in screaming red letters on a yellow background.

McBeth burst into tears. "What have they done to my plans?" she wailed.

Elton tried to calm her down. "It's great!" he said, avoiding the sign problem. "The building looks even better than what you drew."

"But that sign!" McBeth gasped. "It's hideous! Tasteless! *My* plans had the full name of the museum running around the building in subtle earth tones."

"True," said Elton. "Maybe we'd better talk with my dad."

"Welcome home!" shouted Mr. Wazoo when Elton stepped down from the Museummobile and into the driveway. "From your letters, it sounds as though you've found all sorts of ter-rific stuff. Have you seen the building?"

Elton felt slightly embarrassed. "Dad, there's just one thing . . ."

"Oh?"

"That sign. It's kind of . . ."

"Vomitable," McBeth broke in.

Mr. Wazoo nodded sympathetically. "I know. The Town Council made me put it up. They didn't care much for earth tones. They said they wanted something tourists would recognize instantly from blocks away so our residents wouldn't be bombarded with lots of questions about where the museum is."

"Isn't there anything you can do?"

Mr. Wazoo shook his head sadly. "I've tried. The council has the right to order changes in the plans. It's a nice building otherwise, isn't it?"

"It would be perfect," sighed McBeth, "except for that sign. I think I know the solution."

The next morning, a very determined McBeth McBeth stormed into Donati's Donut Den and sat down at the counter. "Welcome home, kid," said Mr. Donati. "What'll it be?"

"I want a donut and coffee," McBeth replied.

"Coffee stunts kids' growth," said Mr. Donati. "What kind of donut? Plain, sugar, chocolate, or jelly?"

"I want a Bavarian cream-filled donut with lingonberry topping and multicolored sprinkles that spell out the word 'delicious.'"

"Ha, ha. Very funny," replied Mr. Donati without laughing. "What'll it be?"

"How about an apricot-fudge donut with green-and-pink frosting and an American flag running around the hole?"

"Come on, kid, I haven't got all day. Plain, sugar, chocolate, or jelly?"

McBeth sat up very straight and gave Mr. Donati a withering stare. "Mr. Donati, I will thank you not to address the co-curator of the First National Drive-Thru Museum and So

Forth as 'kid.' Second, I would like to point out that in our travels across the country, my fellow curator and I have acquired for our collection the very donuts I have just described. Although we originally had planned on exhibiting just one donut, *your* donut, we are beginning to reconsider."

"But the museum promised to show one of my donuts!" Mr. Donati howled.

"Oh, we will, Mr. Donati, we will. And think of it! Think how one of your poor, pitiful, greasy crullers will look beside an Air-Float Chestnut Puff Supreme Special Halloween Decoration Donut—a gorgeous little thing we picked up in Mexico, Maine. Think of the howls of laughter your sad little donut will bring to our visitors."

"You wouldn't do that to me! Would you?"

"I don't see how we can possibly avoid it," McBeth said, pausing dramatically. "Unless . . ."

"Unless?"

McBeth tapped on the counter impatiently. "May I please have that coffee I ordered? And a jelly donut?"

Mr. Donati nervously filled a cup and set it in front of her. "Don't blame me if you grow up short." He slapped a jelly donut onto a plate and slid it down the counter.

"Thank you," said McBeth, dunking daintily.

48

"Unless?" Mr. Donati repeated.

"Unless that hideous sign comes down from the top of the museum," said McBeth with her mouth full.

"Hideous? I think it's kind of tasteful."

"It's about as tasteful as fried maggot stew," said McBeth, "and unless it comes down, we are going to exhibit your donut right next to donuts the likes of which you've never dreamed of."

Mr. Donati turned green. "I'll bring it up at tonight's council meeting."

The sign was gone by noon the next day.

9

McBeth and Elton worked day and night filling the display cases with scale-model San Francisco cable-car cable and Mississippi River mud and Vermont maple syrup and Kentucky bluegrass banjo picks. Each of the hundreds of items they'd acquired in their travels had to be labeled and placed in exactly the proper setting. Deciding how to do that wasn't always easy.

Did the horse collar from Babbs, Oklahoma, belong with the souvenir oil derrick from Oklahoma City, or would it go better beside the pony-ride sign from the Philadelphia Zoo? Would the coffee mug with a picture of Pittsburgh's steel mills fit right in with the coffeepot from Jake's Old Arizona Cafe, or did it seem more interesting with the beer stein from Pittsburg, Kansas? Such questions provoked plenty of arguments between Elton and McBeth, but they always found some way of settling them. Usually they resorted to flipping McBeth's lucky Canadian penny from Niagara Falls, which generally seemed to make the right decision. In fact, it was right so often that in a secret ceremony one night McBeth and Elton appointed it honorary co-curator.

Meanwhile, under cover of darkness, work crews materialized beside the highways of America, erecting the billboards McBeth had designed. The signs were covered with burlap so no one could peek.

In the clean rest rooms, crack teams of plumbing experts flushed and reflushed the toilets. Locksmiths made sure the coin-operated doors and paper-dispensers opened, shut, and accepted any proper combination of nickels, dimes, and quarters. Downtown, three specially selected officers of the Gerbil Police Department practiced directing traffic to and from the museum. Next thing anyone knew, it was Opening Day.

"Display lights?" asked McBeth, reading from

a list on her clipboard.

Elton flipped a switch. "Check."

"Rest room lights?"

"Check."

"Sign?"

"Check."

"Electric carving knife?"

"You're holding it."

McBeth stared at Elton.

"Check," he said, shaking his head.

"Then that's it. We're all set."

McBeth and Elton took one last look around the deserted museum. Then they rubbed her Canadian penny for good luck and hoped they hadn't forgotten anything.

At exactly eleven A.M. Gerbil Daylight Time, two thousand burlap coverings fluttered down beside the highways of America, revealing garish orange-and-yellow billboards that announced the wonders of the First National Drive-Thru Museum, Etc. At exactly one minute after eleven, the Gerbil High School Roller-Skating Band broke into a rousing rendition of "Roll On, Gerbil!" and led a parade of residents down McGinnity Street. At exactly 11:15, the red, white, and blue float carrying the Town Council and Mr. Wazoo met Elton and McBeth at the museum's front entrance.

Smiling for the TV cameras from Wartchester, the two curators handed the electric carving knife to Mayor Curdle. With great drama, she read from a sheet of paper: "The day our citizens have waited for is here at last! I now declare the First National Drive-Thru Museum of American Sightseeing and Clean Rest Rooms open to the public!"

Mayor Curdle pressed the button on the knife and carved the ribbon. An automatic door glided open, and the float of honored citizens rolled into the museum—followed by the entire Roller-Skating Band, twenty-two kids on bicycles, and every last car in town.

A conveyor belt pulled the cars through, reminding most people of an automatic car wash. But the experience was far more interesting. Even the most skeptical townspeople were impressed. It was as though they were taking all the vacations of their lives, but in five minutes' time. Just as they noticed something wonderful and impressive, they'd spot something even more fascinating up ahead, something important and downright educational—like a donut.

All by itself in a display case, and tastefully set off with colored spotlights, even Mr. Donati's plain donut took on a sparkle and a significance no one had ever before noticed. It was no longer merely a donut. It was—in the words of one Gerbilite who had studied archaeology—an artifact, an object that spoke volumes about the daily life of the town.

A pile of sand on a beach would be just another sandpile. But a sandpile in a display case, labeled with the information that it came from the dunes at Kitty Hawk, where Orville and Wilbur Wright flew their first airplane—this was geography, history, and tourism all rolled into one. Painless, too, because you went by it so fast.

After the final exhibit—an American flag made entirely of Popsicle wrappers—the cars arrived at the underground parking lot. Moving sidewalks whisked all the visitors to the clean rest rooms. All the townsfolk admired their tidiness and reminded themselves how lucky it was that as citizens of Gerbil, they didn't have to pay to use the toilets.

Outside, the happy crowd hoisted McBeth, Elton, and Mr. Wazoo to the top of a truck and gave them three rousing cheers. The people were proud of their new museum, the only one of its kind in the entire world, and many of them rode through for another look. On second viewing they noticed details they had missed: the smiling cow stamped on the pats of butter from Rib Falls, Wisconsin; the lacy yet delicately simple tread pattern on the tractor tire from Akron, Ohio. McBeth and the Wazoos got three more cheers.

Then the whole town waited excitedly beside the entrance. The first visitor from outside Gerbil was to be given a personally escorted tour of the museum, a certificate proclaiming him or her Gerbil's Number One Tourist, and unlimited free use of the clean rest rooms.

Suddenly a blast of irritated honking came from a side street blocked off by a crowd of waiting citizens. Instead of following the policemen's directions and the clearly marked signs pointing the way down McGinnity Street to the museum, Gerbil's first tourist had made a wrong turn somewhere.

"This is a street, not a sidewalk!" bellowed a large man from behind the wheel of a huge station wagon filled with grumpy kids and their frazzled mother. The car's windows and bumpers were covered with stickers from Walla Walla, Washington, and Weeki Wachee, Florida, and everywhere in between, and the New Jersey license plate said **IT'S ME!**

"Let's move it!" shouted the driver, leaning on his horn. Elton and McBeth wondered what they'd done to deserve such obnoxiousness.

"Hey, buddy, where's these here rest rooms?"

the driver yelled at someone, who happened to be Mr. Donati.

"You have to go through the museum first," said the councilman, pointing to the entrance. "Be sure you catch my exhibit." And he handed the man a little card that read "After the museum, stop in at Donati's Donut Den, Home of the Only Donut on Permanent Loan."

The driver tossed the card into the backseat, flicked his turn signal, and honked his horn again. TV cameramen began shoving people aside to get closer to the historic car.

By this time, most of the citizens hoped the car would pass on through town so that Gerbil could honor a tourist who was somewhat more polite. But when Mayor Curdle threw up her hands in dismay, the band conductor mistook it for the signal to start playing. Once he struck up the band, all the mayor could do was formally welcome the pioneer visitors.

Mr. Stempel, the driver, grinned and stopped honking. The rest of the family was pleased and surprised at the honor, except for the two littlest kids, who wanted to know where the rest rooms were. Their father thoughtfully told them to shut up.

Homer Hairdo, Wartchester's most popular TV news personality, was the first to get to the

Stempels after they had toured the museum. "Well, what do you think?" he asked.

"Incredible!" boomed Mr. Stempel, leaning out the car window. "We don't have to vacation one more second! We've seen more in five minutes than we usually see in three weeks. Now we can go back home and grill hot dogs in the backyard and relax the way I always wanted to in the first place." He turned to McBeth. "Where can I buy some stickers?"

"Stickers?" McBeth asked.

"You know. Stickers. For my car."

"We never thought of stickers," Elton admitted.

"You have to have stickers," Mr. Stempel insisted. "How else can people prove where they've been?"

McBeth snapped her elastic glasses-holder in frustration. "I knew we'd forget something."

"Well, never you mind," said Gerbil's Number One Tourist. "I know a good thing when I see one. I'm going to move here and open a sticker shop myself. This museum of yours is going to be a gold mine."

He was right. On Opening Day, seven hundred sixty-eight cars, ninety-three bicycles, thirty-five pairs of roller skates, eighteen skateboards, twelve baby strollers, six wheelchairs, and one plastic tricycle visited the museum. Storekeepers had to stay open late selling donuts and coffee, hamburgers and fries, antacids and aspirin. The Hotel Gerbil had to dust off its NO VACANCY sign for the first time in years. Some enterprising citizens even rented out their spare bedrooms.

Within a week, the crowds grew so large they jammed traffic on McGinnity Street—something that hadn't happened since a truckload of roller-skate wheels had overturned in the middle of town thirty years earlier. It became virtually impossible for Gerbilites to drive to the shopping mall, so they stayed home and saved their money and set up lemonade stands to attract thirsty tourists.

After Labor Day, when kids went back to school, the crowds thinned out a little. Still, every weekend, people from miles around flocked to Gerbil to visit the museum.

"Well, we're on the map now, all right," sighed McBeth McBeth one Saturday morning. She leaned back in her swivel chair and stared out the window of the curators' office at the line of cars creeping up McGinnity Street toward the museum.

"These weekend traffic jams never seem to

quit," said Elton, using his binoculars to get a better view. "Hey! Somebody's opening up another new shop downtown!"

"What kind this time?" McBeth inquired.

"Fudge, it looks like. People are coming out with big hunks of fudge."

"Let's see." McBeth borrowed the binoculars. "Wow, are there ever going to be a lot of fat tourists around here."

"I can't believe all these new stores. Stempel's Stickers, Bernie's Brownies, Connie's Cotton Candy, T-Shirt Town."

"Not to mention Gerbil Gardens. Plus all those places going up in the old cornfields on the way into town. Hamburg Heaven, Fish Fiesta, Orange Otis, Pinball Paradise, and all those motels with plastic palm trees in the parking lots."

"Plus Donati's new East Room with the fancy cigarette machine and the waterfall shaped like a donut. That sort of counts."

"And all those cement mixers roaring through town in the middle of the night on their way to the new housing developments."

"Yeah. Gerbil Acres. Gerbil Manor. Gerbil Estates."

"Those used to be pea patches," McBeth

sighed wistfully. "I wonder if all this progress and prosperity is as wonderful as some people seem to think."

Other Gerbilites often wondered exactly the same thing, but the Town Council never had a single doubt. In honor of the town's new boom, they tore down the old sign at the city limits and put up a huge new one:

WELCOME TO GERBIL
A WONDERFUL PLACE TO VISIT
A STUPENDOUS PLACE TO LIVE

10

So many newcomers moved to Gerbil and the town changed so fast that not even the council was the same for long. In the fall elections, Mr. Stempel ran for mayor against Mrs. Curdle. A month in advance, he and his supporters plastered the town so thoroughly with stickers that there was nowhere anyone could look without seeing the name Stempel stuck on something. There was Stempel on the lampposts, Stempel on the sidewalk, Stempel in the shops, Stempel on the stop signs.

There was even Stempel on Mrs. Curdle for a while. One of the Stempel kids slapped a Model 504 Permanent Hold-Tite Sticker on her forehead one morning, but she frowned about it so

much that the glue came unstuck in three or four days. In her speeches, she urged the voters to "Stick with Curdle," but even that reminded them of Stempel. He won by a landslide.

On his first night as mayor, Stempel made a speech to the council. "Honorable Councilpersons," he began, "we have only begun to make Gerbil famous. I recommend that we start to plan ahead for the coming tourist season. Now, what will bring more people to this town than ever before? Answer: The First Annual Great Gerbil Jubilee and Roundup. Picture it: thousands of eager, free-spending tourists running through the streets of our fair town, chasing gerbils with miniature lariats."

"I don't think gerbils know how to use miniature lariats," Councilman Donati interrupted. "Their fingers aren't long enough or something."

"The people will use the lariats," Mayor Stempel explained. "They'll rope the gerbils around their legs just the way cowboys rope dogies. It'll be something like a rodeo, only better. And our town will be the only one that has anything like it."

"Objection," said Councilwoman Wurf, who had been unhappy with Mayor Stempel ever since she'd found one of his campaign stickers dangling from her prize begonia. "It's bad enough having tourists clog up the streets as it is. We certainly don't need gerbils, too."

"But that's the only way it would work," Mr. Stempel replied. "We certainly couldn't have tourists lassoing other tourists."

"We could if I had any say about it," said Ms. Wurf. "Good way to get rid of 'em."

Mayor Stempel politely ignored her. "Do I hear any further discussion?"

Mr. Donati raised his hand. "Where will we get these gerbils?"

"I've thought of that," said Mayor Stempel. "INTERPETCO will lend them to us."

"Whoa, there!" cried Mr. Wazoo from the audience. "This is certainly news to me. And I'm afraid INTERPETCO has a firm policy about restricting its animals to the confines of its farms and ranches."

"Surely you could make an exception for one day a year," Mr. Stempel suggested. "It's not as if we're planning a gerbil barbecue. All the animals will be rounded up and returned at the end of the day."

"I doubt very much that this rule can be broken, no matter what the reason," said Mr. Wazoo.

"You mean to say you would risk losing the

friendship and goodwill of this fine community over a few measly gerbils?" Mayor Stempel huffed.

Everyone in the room stared at Mr. Wazoo. Suddenly no one seemed to remember INTER-PETCO's generosity in building the museum that had made the town's newfound prosperity possible. Mr. Wazoo looked uncomfortable. "I will ask my superiors at INTERPETCO about it," he said nervously.

"How can you even consider it?" Elton asked him after the meeting. "The whole idea stinks, and it's cruel besides. The gerbils won't enjoy this one bit."

"Yeah! Stupidest thing I've ever heard of in my whole life!" muttered Old Man McGinnity. Lonesome Lucy nodded in agreement.

"You're absolutely right," said Mr. Wazoo. "But I gave my word, so I'll have to consult headquarters. I'm positive they'll say no, and that'll be the end of it."

Mr. Wazoo knew INTERPETCO well. In response to his telegram to the president of the company, Mr. Wazoo received a fortune-cookie fortune that said, "He who eats the radish will see great sight." On the back—headquarters was trying to cut down on the amount of paper it wasted—was a personally scribbled note:

Dear Mr. Wazoo and Gerbil Town Council:
NO!
Irritably yours,
R. Torpor
President, INTERPETCO

Except for Ms. Wurf, the Town Council was terribly disappointed. Councilwoman Heimenweiser, who ran the new fudge shop, proposed a big roller-skate-wheel roundup, but the idea didn't generate much enthusiasm. Still, the summer tourist season was approaching fast. Unless somebody came up with a new idea in a hurry, thousands of people might—perish the thought!—spend their time and money elsewhere.

Then Mr. Donati's son-in-law spoke up. Mr. Donati's son-in-law was an assistant at the gerbil farm's laboratory. One day, he explained, while repairing a broken gerbil-washer, he had accidentally made a momentous discovery. When he snapped a spring back and forth to take it out of the machine, all the gerbils in the room suddenly went wild. Every last gerbil scampered to the front of its cage to see what the noise was. After two years of experimenting, the scientist

Mr. Donati's son-in-law worked for had finally determined that somehow the spring gave off ultrasonic vibrations the gerbils just couldn't get enough of.

From all this came the Gerbil-Getter, a little box that gave off electronic sounds higher than the human ear could detect, but absolutely irresistible to a gerbil. All you had to do was turn it on, and every gerbil within ten miles would rush toward it. So, concluded Mr. Donati's son-in-law, INTERPETCO's objections to the Gerbil Jubilee and Roundup were downright silly. If by some odd chance a few gerbils had gone astray by sundown, somebody could set the Gerbil-Getter in the barn, turn it on, and bring all the gerbils home. Sort of like a mechanical Pied Piper.

Mr. Wazoo stood up. "I'm afraid it's not that simple," he began. Three people in the audience booed him softly. "The Gerbil-Getter is still experimental. It works in laboratory conditions, but we have no idea how the gerbils will react to it away from their homes."

A few hisses rose from the crowd. Mr. Wazoo bravely tried to ignore them. "Besides, INTERPETCO is required by law to certify that its animals are clean and disease-free. If we let our gerbils run around with a bunch of tourists chasing them, there's no telling what kind of illnesses they might contract."

Old Man McGinnity's friend Lucy sneezed in agreement.

"Last but not least, I believe this roundup would be cruel to the sensitive animals themselves. I'm afraid INTERPETCO will not be able to participate."As Mr. Wazoo sat down, there was a smattering of applause from Elton, the McBeth family, Ms. Wurf, and Old Man McGinnity. But it could barely be heard over the booing and hissing from everybody else.

When Mayor Stempel's throat began to get sore, he pounded his gavel and brought the meeting back to order. "Is that all you have to say?" he blustered.

Mr. Wazoo nodded.

"In that case, I hereby propose two resolutions. One, that the council take back Mr. Wazoo's keys to our fair city. And two, despite INTERPETCO's uncalled-for refusal to participate, that we hold the First Annual Great Gerbil Jubilee and Roundup as planned. All in favor?"

Nine "ayes" went up from the council.

"Opposed?"

"Me," said Ms. Wurf. Mr. Donati and two other

council members made ugly faces and stuck out their tongues at her.

"The ayes have it," said Mayor Stempel. "At next week's meeting we will appoint a committee to take charge of the preparations for the Jubilee. Any further business?"

All but one of the other councilpersons pointed toward the audience. The mayor pounded his gavel. "Wazoo? The keys, if you please."

All eyes were on Mr. Wazoo as he dug in his pocket and took the first key off his key ring. With a look of sadness and disgust, he handed it to the mayor.

"As far as the town of Gerbil is concerned, from this day forward, you are Locked Out," Mayor Stempel proclaimed to thunderous applause. "The other key, please."

As Mr. Wazoo wrenched it off his key ring, McBeth whispered in Elton's ear. "Something's going very wrong around here."

Elton could only nod in agreement.

11

As things developed, being Locked Out was not exactly the same as being locked out. Mr. Wazoo could still go downtown any time he felt like it, and he could even use the rest room at ex-Mayor Curdle's gas station if he used the regular key like everybody else.

On the other hand, many of the citizens of Gerbil, especially the newcomers, were a lot less friendly than they had been. People would stop Mr. Wazoo on the street and call him a party pooper. Kids in school shoved Elton around just to let him know how they felt about his dad. McBeth did her best to keep it from getting him down.

Meanwhile, plans for the First Annual Great

Gerbil Jubilee and Roundup kept growing. The whole thing was supposed to take place on the Fourth of July. One highlight would be the citizens' reenactment of the noble history of the town. There would also be a Roller-Skate Marathon and a colossal fireworks show. But the main attraction would be the Great Gerbil Roundup itself.

Early in spring, workers went up and down McGinnity Street stringing up red, white, and blue banners that said:

FIRST ANNUAL
GREAT GERBIL JUBILEE AND ROUNDUP
JULY 4, A MOMENTOUS OCCASION

Streamers also went up on all the roadside billboards that advertised the museum. There was only one minor problem. As far as anyone knew, the town of Gerbil could not count on a single gerbil to show up for the occasion.

"I'm worried," said McBeth thoughtfully as she swung with Elton on his porch swing the day before the big event.

"I'm really worried," said Elton, taking a swig of Interpet Cola—the cola with the taste that snuggles up to you.

"I'm really, really worried," said Mr. Wazoo,

mopping his brow with a handkerchief that had a picture of the museum on it.

Old Man McGinnity calmly rocked back and forth and stroked Lonesome Lucy's fur. "What are you so worried about? Thousands of people will show up for the Great Gerbil Roundup, and the council will fall on its rear end. They don't have a single gerbil to their name."

"That's what bothers me," said Mr. Wazoo, gnawing on three of his fingernails at once.

"Why?" McGinnity snorted. "A Gerbil Roundup without gerbils is no crazier than a lot of the other stuff that's been going on around here lately."

Putting it that way, McGinnity definitely had a point. In the past few months, houses, shops, motels, and restaurants had sprung up like weeds, bringing flooded basements, traffic jams, unsavory characters, and acid indigestion to the town of Gerbil. Something like a Gerbil Roundup without any gerbils seemed to fit right in.

But knowing that did not make McBeth or Elton or Mr. Wazoo any calmer. They slept fitfully, turning and tossing and waking up and turning and tossing again all night long.

Yet they wouldn't have slept at all if they had known what was going on out at the gerbil

farm that night. As the moon went down, Mr. Donati's son-in-law sneaked in and unlocked the latches of every last gerbil cage. Then he went to the lab, picked up the Gerbil-Getter, and took it home.

12

By seven the next morning, traffic was beginning to back up on the roads that led
to Gerbil, and by nine the jam was eight miles
long. In town, frustrated drivers gave up looking
for parking spaces in the streets and forked over
six dollars to park on people's lawns. McGinnity
Street was closed to traffic, but by ten o'clock it
was so crowded with pedestrians that they could
barely squeeze past each other.

Mr. Wazoo just stayed home and worried, but
McBeth and Elton went to their museum offices
before the crowd became a crush. From their
windows, they looked down and saw hordes of
people dressed in rodeo outfits and carrying big

lariats. Other people were dressed in ugly multicolored shirts and had cameras dangling over
their protuberant stomachs. A few people wore
rodeo outfits and ugly multicolored shirts, carried lariats, *and* had cameras.

"They must be planning to lasso gerbils and
take pictures of themselves doing it at the same
time," said Elton, shaking his head.

At ten A.M. the Jubilee Parade began, with the
mayor and council leading the way up McGinnity Street. The Roller-Skating Band was right
behind, followed by a string of floats that in-
cluded a giant American eagle made entirely of
roller-skate wheels and a papier-mâché gerbil
dressed as the Statue of Liberty. McBeth and
Elton scribbled notes to themselves so they'd
remember to acquire these artifacts for the
museum.

At eleven, the historical pageant *From Potatoburg to Prosperity: The Gerbil Story* unfolded on a
stage that had been set up outdoors in the
museum's overflow parking lot. First, the play
recounted the town's humble beginnings as the
village of Potatoburg and its first one hundred
seventy-five years of general sleepiness—with
brief interruptions for such natural disasters as
the Potato Bug Infestation, the Dutch Elm Dis-
ease, and the Mysterious Instant Swamp, por-

trayed by the first-, second-, and third-grade classes.

Next, actors dressed as roller skates and gerbils re-created the opening of the roller-skate-wheel factory and the gerbil farm from which the town had taken its new name. Finally, people in car costumes celebrated the coming of the First National Drive-Thru Museum, and people in dollar-bill costumes portrayed Gerbil's new-found prosperity.

"Not the end, but the beginning of a new era for our fair town," read Mayor Stempel as the Roller-Skating Band broke into its theme, "Roll On, Gerbil." Then it was lunchtime.

Hungry tourists jammed the restaurants and snack bars and grocery stores in hopes of finding something to eat before the Great Gerbil Roundup began. None of the visitors asked themselves the worrisome question McBeth and Elton and Mr. Wazoo had on their minds: "Where are the gerbils going to come from?"

At one o'clock, in the town square across from the museum, the Gerbil Jubilee and Roundup Committee handed out a miniature lasso to everyone present. Mr. Donati announced the rules: At the mayor's signal, everyone would be free to lasso gerbils, but only with the official miniature lariats—and only around the gerbils' legs. The committee would be watching closely. Violators would lose their lariats and be disqualified. At the end of the day, the person who had rounded up the most gerbils would win the grand prize.

McBeth shook her head. "I still don't get it. Where are the gerbils going to come fr . . . uh-oh . . ."

McBeth's eyes answered her question. At that very moment, Mr. Donati's son-in-law marched through an opening in the crowd and set a strange apparatus in the middle of the square.

"Is that . . . ?" asked McBeth.

Elton cringed and nodded. "The Gerbil-Getter."

Mr. Donati's son-in-law fiddled with some knobs and an antenna. Then he threw a switch.

At the farm, twenty thousand gerbils suddenly had one thought on their minds: *Where is that wonderful music?* To the rodents, it was rock, jazz, classical, disco, opera, ballet, and oompah band all rolled into one. Frantically jiggling, squeezing, and gnawing to push open their unlocked cage doors, the gerbils scurried outside.

Eighty-eight seconds later, the crowd heard the patter of little feet. Everyone turned to look. Rushing down McGinnity Street in an uncontrollable swarm that stretched from curb to curb and spilled onto the sidewalks were thousands of half-crazed gerbils. Without a moment's hesitation, the animals picked their way among the tourists' feet and scrambled toward the Gerbil-Getter.

The crowd whistled, whooped, and applauded. Mr. Donati's son-in-law made the sign of the donut with his thumb and forefinger. Everything was going exactly according to plan.

Suddenly the parade of animals stopped. All the gerbils within a ten-mile radius of the Gerbil-Getter were now clustered around the machine. The mayor stood up on the judging platform. "Let the Great Gerbil Roundup begin!" he proclaimed.

Mr. Donati's son-in-law pressed a remote-control switch and turned off the Gerbil-Getter. For a moment, everything was still. The crowd hesitated, waiting to see what the gerbils would do. The animals hesitated, astonished to find themselves in this strange place that didn't look a bit like their old familiar cages and didn't have wonderful music anymore, either.

Suddenly the crowd exploded with whoops, hollers, and rebel yells. Tiny lariats whirled in the air. Except for a few poor animals that froze with fright, the gerbils took off in every direction, desperately looking for safety. As tourists pushed and shoved each other in pursuit of the animals, twenty thousand gerbils ran into stores, down sewers, and up people's legs.

Although Mr. Wazoo had refused to participate, curiosity finally got the better of him, and he made his way downtown. But when he reached McGinnity Street, he found more than he'd bargained for.

His two favorite gerbils, Emily and Bill, were climbing frantically up a telephone pole with a weaselly-looking, lariat-twirling idiot in hot pursuit. Fist fights were breaking out among the crowd. A woman shrieked as the gerbil she had caught gnawed its way through her paper bag and bit her on the thumb. And, worst of all, a three-hundred-fifty-pound man in a tight cowboy outfit stumbled and fell directly on top of the one-and-only Gerbil-Getter.

From their vantage point at the museum, Elton and McBeth saw the machine crumble to bits. Then they saw Mr. Wazoo break down and cry.

13

"What now?" McBeth wondered aloud as she stared in disgust at the commotion in the streets below. As if to answer her, six frightened rodent heads peeked out from under her desk, then slipped back underneath.

"I'm thinking," Elton replied. He'd seen quite a few animal escapes in his time, but none as unusual as this. Once in a while, lions and bears and kangaroos had broken out of INTERPETCO's other facilities, but mostly one at a time. A whole farm of animals on the loose was really quite different. About the only good point was that gerbils weren't man-eating—just man-nipping sometimes when they got upset. But like other rodents, gerbils have a powerful need to gnaw. While the Gerbil-Getter was being repaired (if that was even possible), the gerbils might gnaw away half the town.

Besides his father, who didn't look as though he'd be much help at the moment, Elton could think of only one other gerbil expert in town: Old Man McGinnity. He picked up the phone and dialed McGinnity's number.

"Who are you calling?" McBeth asked.

"Old Man McGinnity."

"He's not home," McBeth informed him. "I just saw him running down the street, hollering, 'Lucy, you come home this instant!'"

Elton sighed and hung up the phone. "Would you say this is an emergency?"

McBeth looked exasperated. "Would you say the sinking of the *Titanic* was an emergency?"

Elton dug into his wallet, pulled out a card, and showed it to her. **FOR EMERGENCY USE ONLY**, it read. **WILL ROUND UP STRAY ANIMALS**. It was battered but thick, something like a cardboard credit card.

"Use it!" McBeth cried. "Hurry!"

Elton read the card. "One: Hold card between thumb and forefinger of right hand." Elton did.

"Two: Cross middle finger and index finger of left hand." Elton did.

"Three: With a downward motion, use right

hand to flick card against crossed fingers." Elton did. Nothing happened.

He tried again. Still nothing.

"You haven't even lured the gerbils out from under the desk," said McBeth. "Let me try."

Elton handed her the card. She followed the instructions exactly, flicking slowly at first, then faster and faster. It didn't work at all.

"Maybe this card's out of order," McBeth said, handing it back to Elton. "It's all scratched and banged up from being in your wallet."

Elton looked out the window at the chaos below. He wished the gerbils could somehow grab the lariats and use them on the tourists, but he knew that would be highly unlikely. "Time for step four," he declared.

McBeth looked at the back of the card. "Four: If card fails to get results, phone me immediately. Love, Mom."

Elton knew his mother was the only person in the world who would know how to put an end to this insanity. He dug into his wallet again, took out another card, picked up the phone, and dialed the operator. "I want to call Tasmania. The number is KOala 8382."

The operator laughed. "Kid, is this some kind of gag?"

"It's no gag. It's an emergency."

"What kind of emergency needs help from Tas—eek!" The line went dead for a second. "Help!" shrieked the operator.

"That's the emergency!" Elton replied. "The town is crawling with gerbils!"

"Okay, kid, stay on the line. If I can get these crazy animals to quit running all over my switchboard, I'll put your call through. Whoops! One of them just bit the cord to my headset."

"Hurry!" Elton pleaded.

The operator worked as fast as he could. He punched some buttons, flashing an electronic signal from Gerbil to a computer in Wilkes-Barre, Pennsylvania. At the speed of light, the signal traveled to Ronkonkoma, New York, zipped from a giant antenna to a space satellite twenty-five thousand miles from earth, sped down to an antenna in Tasmania, and shot across a wire through the countryside, ringing the phone in Mrs. Wazoo's temporary residence, where it was the middle of winter and four o'clock the next morning. A groggy voice answered. At the speed of light, it made the return trip to Gerbil, Pennsylvania.

"Hello?" Elton heard the voice say.

"This is Elton Wazoo. Could I speak to my mother? It's an emergency."

Even at the speed of light, his words took a

couple of seconds to get to Tasmania. The answer took a couple more to return. "She's not here. She's . . ."

The line went dead. "Hello? Hello?" Elton shouted, but it was no use. McBeth pointed out the window. A team of frantic, hungry gerbils had gnawed through the main telephone line to the building. Elton groaned and hung up the phone.

What else was going on at that moment? Getting into the spirit of the celebration, tourists were twirling their miniature lariats all over town, much to the dismay of the townspeople. Ms. Wurf ran home and found three gerbils munching on her prize begonia while three clumsy tourists took aim at the rodents for the fourteenth time.

Mr. Donati rushed to his Donut Den and found gerbils having a donut feast and frolicking in his waterfall. Mayor Stempel waddled to his store as fast as he could and learned that gerbils found the adhesive backing of stickers a rare and tasty delicacy. Down in the museum, gerbils were creating a disaster area as they turned the exhibits into playgrounds and munched on their most delicious ingredients. At the curb of McGinnity Street, Mr. Wazoo hid his face in his hands, peeking out between his fingers just long enough to convince himself that the town, the farm, and his life were utterly ruined.

It didn't seem to have much to do with the action below, but suddenly a red, white, and blue helicopter appeared in the sky and descended toward the roof of the museum. In the middle of the fuss, uproar, and commotion, Elton and McBeth were the only ones who noticed.

14

With their special key, Elton and McBeth unlocked the stairway and clambered up to the roof. The helicopter touched down. Its blades whirled to a halt. A tall woman in safari pants and a bush jacket jumped out, her long, dark hair fluttering in the breeze.

"Mom!" Elton exclaimed, running toward her. "Am I ever glad to see you!"

The hugs and kisses and mushy stuff were over in a few seconds. Then Elton introduced McBeth. She and Mrs. Wazoo had heard a lot about each other.

"I decided to surprise you and drop in for a Fourth of July picnic and get-together," Mrs.

Wazoo told her son. "Nobody was home, so I came here. Where's your father?"

Elton handed her his binoculars and pointed. "He's the one with his hands over his eyes."

"He certainly doesn't look any too happy," said Mrs. Wazoo, bringing the field glasses into sharper focus. "Wait a minute! There are gerbils climbing up his neck!"

Elton nodded grimly. "We have a little problem here."

"I'll say!" said McBeth. She and Elton quickly told Mrs. Wazoo the whole sad history of the Great Gerbil Jubilee and Roundup.

"By the way, your emergency card didn't work," Elton said.

"Of course not," replied his mom. "It won't work on more than four large animals or eight small ones at a time. It's not powerful enough for a job like this."

Just then, sixteen gerbils scurried across the roof and began gnawing on the helicopter seats. Elton's mom stuck her left index finger in her mouth, puffed up her left cheek, and tapped on it gently with the palm of her other hand. Ten seconds later, fifteen gerbils stood at attention at her feet, and the sixteenth climbed up and gave her a kiss.

"Wow!" exclaimed McBeth.

"I told you," Elton said proudly. "Nobody has a way with animals like Mom."

"Can you round up all the gerbils?" McBeth asked her.

"Not while people are running all over town chasing them. We'll have to get rid of all the tourists first."

"How?"

"To catch an animal, you have to think like an animal. To snare a tourist, you have to think like a tourist. What's the one thing that frightens vacationers more than anything else?"

"I give up," said McBeth.

"Bad weather," Mrs. Wazoo declared. "Let a thunderstorm churn up, and tourists will disappear. And it so happens that my helicopter comes equipped with the 'Stormy Weather' cloud-seeding attachment for producing downpours."

Elton looked up. "I hate to mention this, but there's not a cloud in the sky."

Mrs. Wazoo frowned. "Well, we'll have to try another approach. What attracts tourists more than anything else?"

"That's easy," said McBeth. "Cheap food. All you have to do is dangle a five-cent hot dog before a tourist's eyes, and he'll snap at it."

"Where are we going to get five-cent hot dogs?" Elton wondered.

"We aren't. We're just going to advertise them," said Mrs. Wazoo.

"How? All the tourists are too busy chasing gerbils to pay attention."

"This particular helicopter also comes equipped with the 'All-Purpose Drive-'Em-Nuts Advertising Kit.' It has everything you need for effective advertising by air. Come on."

Elton and McBeth helped Mrs. Wazoo set up a special wiener-shaped balloon with lettering that read **HOT DOGS! FIVE CENTS! FOLLOW ME!** Next, all three of them yelled at once to make a tape recording that said the same thing. Then they took off, flying just above the heads of the whooping, lasso-twirling crowd. Nobody even bothered to look up.

"Press the blue button!" Mrs. Wazoo shouted. Elton did.

The wiener-shaped balloon behind them suddenly inflated and lit up. From the giant speakers on either side of the helicopter blared five hundred watts of sheer noise power. "Hot Dogs! Five Cents! Follow Me!" repeated over and over. It sounded (because of special electronic cir-

cuitry) not like Elton, McBeth, and Mrs. Wazoo, but like the Voice of Doom.

The scene suddenly changed. Somebody below would be twirling his lasso with every last ounce of twirl he could muster. An instant later, he or she would freeze in mid-twirl, look up at the giant flying frankfurter, and start following it. Within minutes, a line formed beneath the helicopter. Tourists who had been busy chasing gerbils in unlikely places stuck their heads out from trees and drainpipes and manholes and ran toward their cars, always keeping one eye on the enormous wienie.

Mrs. Wazoo buzzed the town again to make sure she'd gotten her message across to every last tourist. Then she cranked up the sound and led the parade of cars down the highway out of town.

Ten miles past the town limits, she pressed a green button that cut the frankfurter balloon adrift. It kept flying along the road, and the cars kept following it.

Mrs. Wazoo banked the helicopter and headed back toward Gerbil. "That balloon's got quite a range," she said. "By the time those tourists know they've been tricked, they'll be at the Wartchester Mall, too tired and too hungry to think of coming back here. Now let's have a roundup of our own."

Flying over town, they saw the tourist-free hamlet spring back to life. As harried citizens flushed gerbils out of vegetable patches, flower beds, compost heaps, and kitchens, Mrs. Wazoo grasped the control stick with her knees. "Hold the microphone up to my mouth," she told Elton. "And press the button."

As Elton held the microphone up close, Mrs. Wazoo stuck her left index finger in her mouth, puffed up her left cheek, and tapped on it with the palm of her right hand. From the speakers blasted five hundred deafening watts of a strange sound that meant absolutely nothing to humans—except maybe that they ought to put their hands over their ears.

But to the gerbils, the sound said, "Follow me, and I will show you something wonderful." It said, "Hurry!" It said, "Don't be left behind!" It was even more irresistible than the sound of the Gerbil-Getter or an offer of five-cent hot dogs.

Little scurrying tricklets of gerbils down below turned into rivers of gerbils that turned into a thundering gerbil ocean. Gerbils clambered out of chimneys, gutters, and barbecues and followed the helicopter to the farm. Mr. Wazoo ran along behind them to make sure they didn't decide to turn back.

As the copter hovered over the barn, twenty thousand gerbils stood on the threshold and looked up toward the marvelous sound. They dimly remembered that this familiar-looking place was home, but they were more interested in the beautiful sounds overhead.

Then Mrs. Wazoo turned off the helicopter's loudspeakers, and the animals caught sight of Mr. Wazoo. Instantly realizing where they were, the gerbils scampered into their cages in less than a minute.

Mrs. Wazoo quickly landed the helicopter and ran inside with Elton and McBeth to help lock the cage doors. Mr. Wazoo gave his favorite gerbils, Emily and Bill, a warm caress. Elton's father and mother gave each other a big hug and kiss, the kind people give each other when they haven't been together in a very long time. Then everybody collapsed in the middle of the floor.

Mayor Stempel and the rest of the Town Council slinked into the barn. "Are they all captured?" squeaked the mayor. "Are they all in their cages?"

Mr. Wazoo nodded wearily.

"And the tourists? They're gone for good?"

"I can almost guarantee it," said Mrs. Wazoo.

"Mayor Stempel and fellow councilpersons, allow me to introduce my wife, Edie," said Elton's dad. "If it weren't for her, we'd still be in quite a pickle."

Mayor Stempel bowed politely. He took out his handkerchief and mopped his dripping brow. "I guess everything's all right, then," he said. "This whole celebration seems to have gotten a little out of hand."

McBeth knew she should keep her mouth shut, but she just couldn't resist. "Some people told you that a long time ago." The mayor winced.

"And everything's *not* all right," Mr. Wazoo pointed out. "Who's going to pay for the tests to make sure the gerbils are clean and healthy? Who's going to pay for all the damage the tourists and gerbils caused?"

"Those are your gerbils, Wazoo!" the mayor blustered. "If you can't keep them locked up and under control, maybe the council will have to ban gerbils from the area."

"Oh, don't be a jerk, Stempel," said Ms. Wurf, whose prize begonia had died of fright. "Everybody knows you paid Mr. Donati's son-in-law to unlock the cages and steal the Gerbil-Getter. I think the very least the council can do is apologize for the way it acted."

The mayor looked very embarrassed.

"Well, do it, you big fool, before the rest of us beat you to it," Ms. Wurf insisted.

"I'm sorry," said the mayor, biting his lip and turning bright red.

"We're all sorry," said Mr. Donati. "My son-in-law never wants to look at another gerbil. But I'll bet you don't ever want to look at my son-in-law again."

Mr. Wazoo nodded as politely as he could under the circumstances.

"I know exactly how you must feel," said Mr. Donati. "So I'm taking him into the donut business. This way, he'll have a hole life ahead of him. Get it? A hole life?"

Mr. Wazoo nodded again. Then a shout burst through the door, followed by a person.

"Lucy! You in here? Come to Papa!" hollered Old Man McGinnity. He shook his fist at Mayor Stempel and bellowed, "Why, you old gerbil-hater, if those lasso-toting idiots of yours harmed one hair of Lucy's hide, I'll—"

Fortunately, he never had to finish the sentence. Lonesome Lucy popped out from behind a water cooler, scampered up Mayor Stempel's leg, nipped his earlobe, and leaped happily to McGinnity's shoulder.

"Now, here's an animal with the smarts," said

the old man, stalking out the door. "The rest of you I'm not so sure about." No one dared to disagree.

Then, shoved slightly by Ms. Wurf and Mr. Donati, Mayor Stempel stepped forward again. "In appreciation of your services, Mrs. Wazoo, I hereby declare you winner of the First Annual Great Gerbil Jubilee and Roundup."

"*Last* Annual, I hope," said Mrs. Wazoo. "What do I win?"

Mayor Stempel looked embarrassed again.

"Well, tell her!" demanded Ms. Wurf. "Go ahead!"

Mayor Stempel had trouble getting the words out. "It's a . . . that is . . . well, a trophy . . . a gold-plated replica . . . of a . . . well, a miniature . . . uh, lariat."

"I can hardly find the words to express my thanks," said Mrs. Wazoo.

15

Elton and McBeth led everyone to the museum, and McBeth's parents joined them on the way. The damage in the exhibit area was worse than anyone could have imagined. Either the Eternallife Preservative had failed or the gerbils had found it tasty. Every bit of food in the display cases had been gnawed to a nub. Four well-trampled meat patties were all that remained of the vegetarian rodents' attack on a quadruple-decker Texasburger. The perfect Silver Dollar Pancake was now smaller than a dime. And all that was left of Mr. Donati's donut was the hole.

"Look at this!" cried McBeth, shaking her head in horror. "They ate their way through three-quarters of our matchbook collection!"

"And our display of educational placemats and pictorial sugar packets!" groaned Elton. "They can never be replaced!"

"We're ruined," sighed McBeth. "Even the rest rooms are a mess."

"Fellow councilpersons," thundered the mayor, "I move we declare the museum a disaster area and offer it all our support to help get it back on its feet again as soon as possible."

"Not so fast, Stempel!" cried Ms. Wurf. "The rest of us have been discussing this on the way over here. We're not too sure we care if we ever see another tourist in this town. We're beginning to think this museum should be shut down for good."

"But what will become of this beautiful building?" spluttered Stempel, thinking of all the money he had tied up in stickers with the museum's name on them. "What will become of the town?"

"The town will probably go back to being pretty much what it was before the museum opened, which is fine with most of us," Ms. Wurf declared. "As for the building, I think it would make a wonderful playground, roller-skating rink, public comfort station, recreation center, and car wash. Any objections?"

Mr. Wazoo realized he'd done his best to put Gerbil on the map, and he was sure INTER-PETCO wouldn't mind donating the building to the town for such a good cause, so he didn't object. Elton and McBeth were sad to see their brilliant museum go down the drain, but they really couldn't see any way around it, so they didn't object. And Mr. Stempel was afraid of what the others might do to him if he objected, so he didn't, either.

"All in favor?" said Ms. Wurf.

A chorus of "ayes" went up. A few of the councilpersons thought they even heard a little squeak from Mayor Stempel, but no one could say for sure.

"All opposed?"

Silence.

"The ayes have it. Mayor Stempel, please declare the First National Drive-Thru Museum of American Sight Seeing and Clean Rest Rooms officially closed for remodeling into the Gerbil Community Center, Roller Rink, and Car Wash."

Mayor Stempel did just that. "Anybody want to buy some valuable souvenirs of the good old days?" he asked afterward. "I can give you a real good deal on stickers."

Nobody took him up on the offer.

"Well," said McBeth, "it was fun while it lasted."

"Yeah," Elton agreed. "But I bet we'll hear plenty about this from the kids at school." He could almost feel himself being kicked around again.

"Wait a second! I nearly forgot!" said Mrs. Wazoo. "You're not going back to school here."

"What?" cried Elton.

"In all the hubbub, it slipped my mind," his mom explained. "We've been reassigned to Africa. They've transferred us to the INTERPETCO offices at Victoria Falls."

"Us? Both of us? At the same time?" Mr. Wazoo asked.

Mrs. Wazoo nodded. "Isn't it wonderful?"

Mr. Wazoo gave her a big hug.

"Boy, are you lucky," McBeth told Elton. "Victoria Falls is almost twice as big as Niagara. You have to be the luckiest kid in the world."

"Oh, by the way," Elton's mom told Mr. Wazoo with a mischievous gleam in her eye, "headquarters said you should bring along two of your top animal keepers if possible. And I've been searching everywhere for an apprentice animal trainer."

McBeth couldn't help but overhear. "My parents are terrific animal keepers," she told

Elton's mom. "What kind of animals do you raise at Victoria Falls?"

Mrs. Wazoo grinned. "What kind would you expect to find at Rory Rallickson's Rhinoceros Ranch Number Two?"

McBeth McBeth jumped in the air so wildly her elastic band sent her glasses across the room like a slingshot.

"Search no more!" she cried, blind but overjoyed.

Three days later, two huge INTERPETCO motor homes rolled down McGinnity Street with Mr. Wazoo and Elton in one and Joe and Lady Bird McBeth in the other. Mrs. Wazoo and her new apprentice, McBeth, flew ahead in the helicopter.

Near the outskirts of Gerbil, a huge station wagon with a large man, a bunch of grumpy kids, a frazzled mother, lots of luggage, and a Pennsylvania license plate that said **STICKERS** roared past the motor homes in a big hurry to get out of town. It was just at that moment that Elton noticed a brand-new sign by the side of the road:

**YOU ARE NOW DEPARTING GERBIL
AN OKAY PLACE TO LEAVE**